It was home time. Ollie and Emma
were waiting by the school door.

Mrs Bootle came up. "Your mum phoned," she said. "She's running late so you can wait with me."

4

Mrs Bootle was sorting out the boot box, where the lost boots were kept. "Just look," she said. "There's no name inside any of these boots."

Ollie and Emma stared.
There were old boots and
new boots, small boots and
tall boots, bright boots and
dull boots, and boots with
patterns on.

Who had left the boots at school?
Some were just dropped.

Some were left behind at
holiday times.

Some were left behind when
children went off to new schools.

They dropped the oldest boots
into a recycling bag.
"It seems a pity to get rid of these
other boots," said Emma.

"What else can we do?" replied Mrs Bootle. "Nobody will want to wear them."

Mum arrived. She held a tray of young plants. "Sorry I'm late, Mrs Bootle. Please have these," she said. "Put them into some pots somewhere in the school."

"But the school hasn't got any flowerpots," said Mrs Bootle.

Ollie and Emma looked at the plants, and they looked at the boots. Then they smiled. "But the school does have lots of boots," they said.

"It certainly does!" said Mrs Bootle. "And I think tomorrow will be a busy day for us."

Next morning, the boots were
washed clean inside and out.

When the boots were dry, Emma,
Ollie and their friends made them
look good. Mrs Bootle put small
holes in the boots.

The next day, the children filled the boots with grit and good earth.

Then they planted tiny plants in each boot.

Last of all, they watered
the boots well.

The children set the boot-pots in
rows outside the school. Tiny green
shoots peeped out of each one.

"The plants look rather small," said Ollie.

"They'll grow soon," said Emma.

The sun shone down on the boots for some of the day. The little plants grew stronger.

Everyone took it in turns to
water the plants.

Before long, the plants grew strong
stems and leaves and buds.
Some plants climbed up
the school wall.

Then, one sunny day, the flowers opened and spread their bright petals.

Mrs Bootle looked very happy.
"Our school looks very cheerful
now," she said.

"Aren't you glad we had so many lost boots, Mrs Bootle?" laughed Ollie and Emma.

29

Puzzle 1

Put these pictures in the correct order.
Now try writing the story in your own words!

Puzzle 2

1. I'm sorry. I was held up at work.

2. We could use the boots as flowerpots!

3. Wait with me, children!

4. Could you plant these at school?

5. It's lucky we had the boots after all!

6. Today, class, we are making pots.

Choose the correct speech bubbles for the characters. Can you think of any others? Turn over to find the answers.

Answers

Puzzle 1

The correct order is: 1e, 2d, 3f, 4a, 5c, 6b

Puzzle 2

Mrs Bootle: 3, 6

Ollie and Emma: 2, 5

Mum: 1, 4

Look out for more great Hopscotch stories:

AbracaDebra
ISBN 978 0 7496 9427 2*
ISBN 978 0 7496 9432 6

Bless You!
ISBN 978 0 7496 9429 6*
ISBN 978 0 7496 9434 0

Marigold's Bad Hair Day
ISBN 978 0 7496 9430 2*
ISBN 978 0 7496 9435 7

My Dad's a Balloon
ISBN 978 0 7496 9428 9*
ISBN 978 0 7496 9433 3

How to Teach a Dragon Manners
ISBN 978 0 7496 5873 1

The Best Den Ever
ISBN 978 0 7496 5876 2

The Princess and the Frog
ISBN 978 0 7496 5129 9

I Can't Stand It!
ISBN 978 0 7496 5765 9

The Truth about those Billy Goats
ISBN 978 0 7496 5766 6

Izzie's Idea
ISBN 978 0 7496 5334 7

Clever Cat
ISBN 978 0 7496 5131 2

"Sausages!"
ISBN 978 0 7496 4707 0

The Truth about Hansel and Gretel
ISBN 978 0 7496 4708 7

The Queen's Dragon
ISBN 978 0 7496 4618 9

Plip and Plop
ISBN 978 0 7496 4620 2

Find out more about all the Hopscotch books at:
www.franklinwatts.co.uk

*hardback